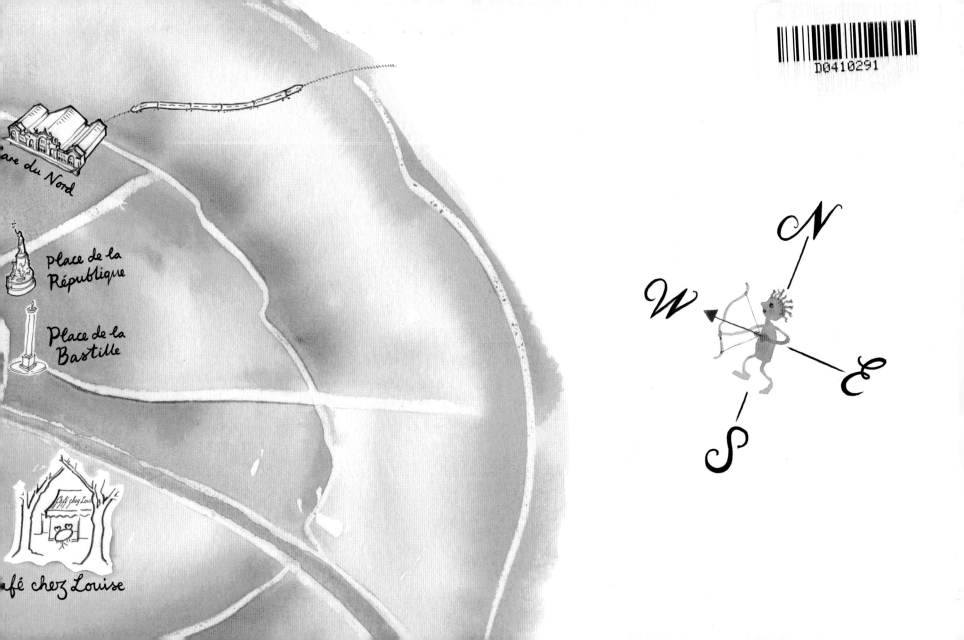

Gare du Nord

Place de la
République

Place de la
Bastille

Café chez Louise

Café chez Louise

D0410291

N

W

E

S

First published in Great Britain in 2008 by

Quercus
21 Bloomsbury Square
London
WC1A 2NS

Text copyright © Carolyn Hink, 2008
Illustrations copyright © Emma Calder, 2008

The moral right of Carolyn Hink and Emma Calder to be
identified as the author and illustrator of this work has
been asserted in accordance with the Copyright,
Design and Patents Act, 1988.

All rights reserved. No part of this publication may be reproduced
or transmitted in any form or by any means, electronic or mechanical,
including photocopy, recording, or any information storage and retrieval
system, without permission in writing from the publisher.

A CIP catalogue reference for this book is available
from the British Library

ISBN 978 1 84724 435 2

This book is a work of fiction. Names, characters, businesses, organizations,
places and events are either the product of the author's imagination or are
used fictitiously. Any resemblance to actual persons, living or dead,
events or locales is entirely coincidental.

10 9 8 7 6 5 4 3 2 1

Printed and bound in China

Miss Louise goes to
PARIS

To Vita, the real Miss Louise,
and all teachers who look after other
people's children with love and kindness,
Carolyn

To Julian with love,
Emma

Written by Carolyn Hink
Illustrated by Emma Calder

Miss Louise goes to PARIS

Quercus

Miss Louise is my teacher. She is lovely and kind.

She went to Paris in the holidays. It was her boyfriend's Valentine's present to her.

♥ euroheart

Miss Louise

Date	Time	Depart ⟶	Arrive	Date	Time
14 Feb	07h09	LONDON	PARIS	14 Feb	10h59

TRAIN   LUV   Coach 2   Seat 12

Price   £ xxx.xx

I don't really know what Valentine's Day is.

I asked my big brother. He told me
it's all about sweethearts and kissing.

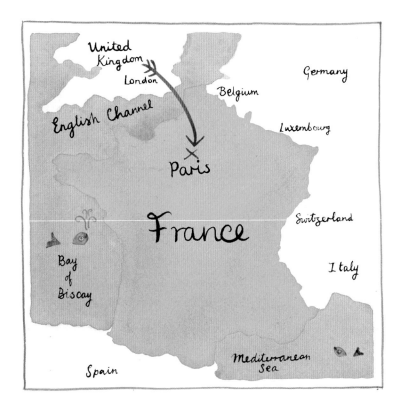

Miss Louise went to Paris by train. Paris is in France. She said the train goes very fast.

 LONDON

There is water between England and France and the train goes underneath it through a tunnel, my brother says.

PARIS

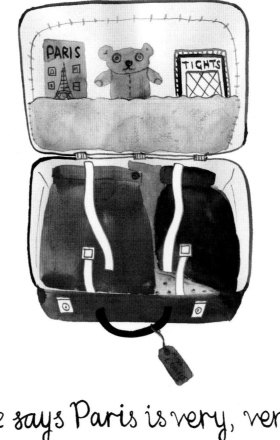

Miss Louise says Paris is very, very beautiful.
She says she took her bag to the hotel and
changed into a skirt. This was very Parisian.

la grenouille

un camion

l'artiste

METROPOLITAIN

Bonjour!

Tour Eiffel

le garçon

les sucettes

les escargots

une glace

The train goes through the tunnel and then
it's in Paris. They speak French in Paris.
I am learning to speak French.

un chat

le Vélo

mon frère

Then she and her boyfriend went for a walk through the streets. They walked and walked and walked. The streets in Paris are wide and long. They are called boulevards and have huge trees along the sides.

Miss Louise and her boyfriend stopped for a coffee in a café where they sat outside and watched the people walk by.

She noticed the people in the cafés talked a lot, they all looked very chic and serious.

They left the café and walked
along the river that flows through Paris.
It's called the Seine. People sell books on the
riverbank, out of black hanging boxes.

Miss Louise bought a book from the old
days with black and white pictures of Paris.

They walked to a tower called the Eiffel Tower.

A
lift
took them
up to the
top
so that

they
could
look
down
and
see
Paris.

She said it was freezing cold and very windy.

They walked around the top and looked at Paris, which looked very neat and tidy and clean from so high up, to see if they could find their hotel.

Then Miss Louise's boyfriend pulled her around to the side that was less windy and he got down on his knees and held her hands.

She looked down at him and he looked
at her and then he asked her to marry him.
Everyone around them pretended to be
looking at Paris. But really they were all
looking at him and her and everyone waited.

My brother says you only go down on ONE knee when you ask someone to marry you and how embarrassing for them in front of all those people. I don't see what the difference is on one knee or on two and I don't think it's embarrassing either.

She pulled him up and whispered her answer into his ear.

I asked her what her answer was
and she smiled and showed me her hand.
It had a twinkling ring on it.

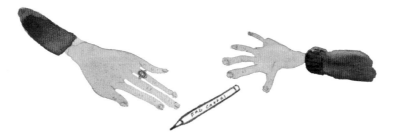

I think she is going to marry him.

I hope I can go to Paris.
I want to walk around its beautiful boulevards
wearing a skirt and imagine something magical
will happen to me.

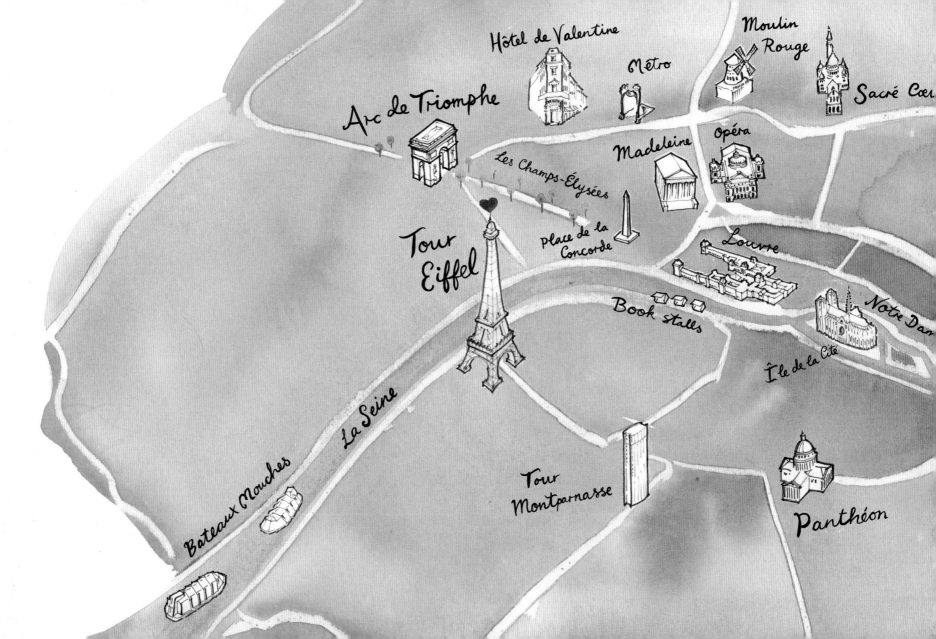

Hôtel de Valentine

Moulin Rouge

Métro

Sacré Cœr

Arc de Triomphe

Madeleine

Opéra

Les Champs-Élysées

Place de la Concorde

Tour Eiffel

Louvre

Book stalls

Notre Dam

Île de la Cité

La Seine

Tour Montparnasse

Panthéon

Bateaux Mouches